MR TIDDLES
CAT BURGLAR

For Claire, Joe & Harry, with love.
And remembering Billy,
the original Mr Tiddles.
TM

SIMON & SCHUSTER
First published in Great Britain in 2012
by Simon & Schuster UK Ltd
1st Floor, 222 Gray's Inn Road, London, WC1X 8HB

This paperback edition first published in 2022

A CIP catalogue record for this book is available from the British Library upon request

ISBN: 978-1-3985-1310-5 (PB)
ISBN: 978-0-85707-720-2 (eBook)
Printed in China
10 9 8 7 6 5 4 3 2 1

MR TIDDLES CAT BURGLAR

Tom McLaughlin

SIMON & SCHUSTER
London New York Sydney Toronto New Delhi

For as long as he could remember, all Harry had wanted in the whole wide world was a cat – a furry-purry friend to care for and to play with.

And you'll never guess what . . .

This was Harry's lucky day.
Today was Harry's birthday
and a cat is just what he got!

"What a perfect pusscat!"
said Harry, excitedly.
"I'll call him Mr Tiddles."

Every day, Harry made sure that Mr Tiddles
was as happy as a cat could possibly be.

Every night, he tucked Mr Tiddles up on the comfiest armchair and stroked his tummy until he drifted into a dreamy sleep.

Harry LOVED his new friend.

Mr Tiddles loved Harry, too, and he wanted to show him how lucky he was to have such a kind friend.

First he brought Harry a fresh mouse.

But Harry just went a funny colour.

Then he left Harry's favourite treat at the bottom of his bed –

triple chocolate
cream-and-custard cake
with extra banana jam!

"Mmmm, delicious,"
said Harry, as he licked
a dollop of cream. "But
where did this come from?"

Mr Tiddles kept quiet.

The next day, Harry found a pogo stick, and a train tooting its way around his bedroom. "What's going on? Where has all this come from?" he cried.
Mr Tiddles just grinned.

Day by day things got even more puzzling. Before long Harry's room was awash with rockstar guitars, peculiar paintings, fearsome dinosaurs, yummy jelly beans and whooshing jet packs.

Campbell's
Tomato
soup
wanted

Then, one morning, Harry awoke to
find a horse named Alan in his bedroom!

It was the last straw!

“What are you up to, Mr Tiddles,
you rascally cat?” he cried.

Mr Tiddles didn't make a sound.
He just went a little red in the face.

What mischief was Mr Tiddles
getting up to while Harry was asleep?

That evening, Harry followed Mr Tiddles as he vanished into the night, slinking along high wires, leaping across rooftops and jumping over rickety fences. It was a job for Harry to keep up,

UNTIL . . .

SPACE CENTRE
toy shop
Museum
opera house
Old west Ranch

Mr Tiddles reached the home of THE QUEEN!
"Oh, my!" said Harry, as the rascally moggy squeezed through the railings and started to scale the wall. "Mr Tiddles is a cat burglar! HOW DIABOLICAL!"

Taking a deep breath, Harry followed Mr Tiddles . . .

over the palace gates,

up the palace wall,

and into the royal bedroom.

"STOP!" shouted Harry–
just as Mr Tiddles swiped the crown right off the royal head.

Mr Tiddles froze,
the Queen woke up,
and Harry started to fall!
"Heeeeelp!" he screamed.

WHOOOOSH!
Quick as a flash, Mr Tiddles dropped the royal crown
and dived across the room.

Aaarghh!

With a swish and a swoop, and some splendid acrobatics, Mr Tiddles grabbed Harry's shoelace and hauled him back through the window.

"Phew! That was close!" sighed Harry, as he and Mr Tiddles landed in a heap at the Queen's slippers.

The Queen, however, was not amused. “Guards!” she called. “Arrest these two intruders for Acts of Cheekiness Against the Crown.”

"No!" cried Harry. "Please, your Majesty, Mr Tiddles isn't a bad cat. He's just been taking things because he cares for me so much."

"You mean, he's stolen other things, too?" cried the Queen in dismay.

She scratched her royal head and a royal thought popped into her royal brain. "It's wrong to steal," she snorted. "But I think Mr Tiddles has learned his lesson. I can see that he isn't a bad cat. If he promises to give everything back, we'll say no more about it."

Mr Tiddles looked up at the Queen and gave the cutest furry-purry pussycat smile that he could muster.

With no time to lose, Mr Tiddles returned the grand piano to the conductor at the Opera House . . .

the whooshing jet pack to the astronaut,

the noisy guitar to the rockstar man,

and Alan to a very relieved cowboy.

When they were finished, Harry gave
Mr Tiddles his biggest, bestest squeezy-hug.

The two of them agreed, then and there, that having
each other was the best present anyone could wish for.

THE END